50

Happy Birthday Bugs

Bugs 50th logo is a trademark of Warner Bros. Inc. © 1990

This Looney Tunes Library Book is published by Longmeadow Press
201 High Ridge Road, Stamford, CT 06904
in association with Sammis Publishing

With special thanks to

Guy Gilchrist • Gill Fox • Tom Brenner • Marie Gilchrist
Brad Gilchrist • Jim Bresnahan • Rich Montesanto • John Cacanindin
Ron Venancio • Norma Rivera • Allan Mogel • Gary A. Lewis

Printed in the United States of America
0 9 8 7 6 5 4 3 2 1

BUGS BUNNY *and* ELMER FUDD
in NIGHTY NIGHT, BUGS

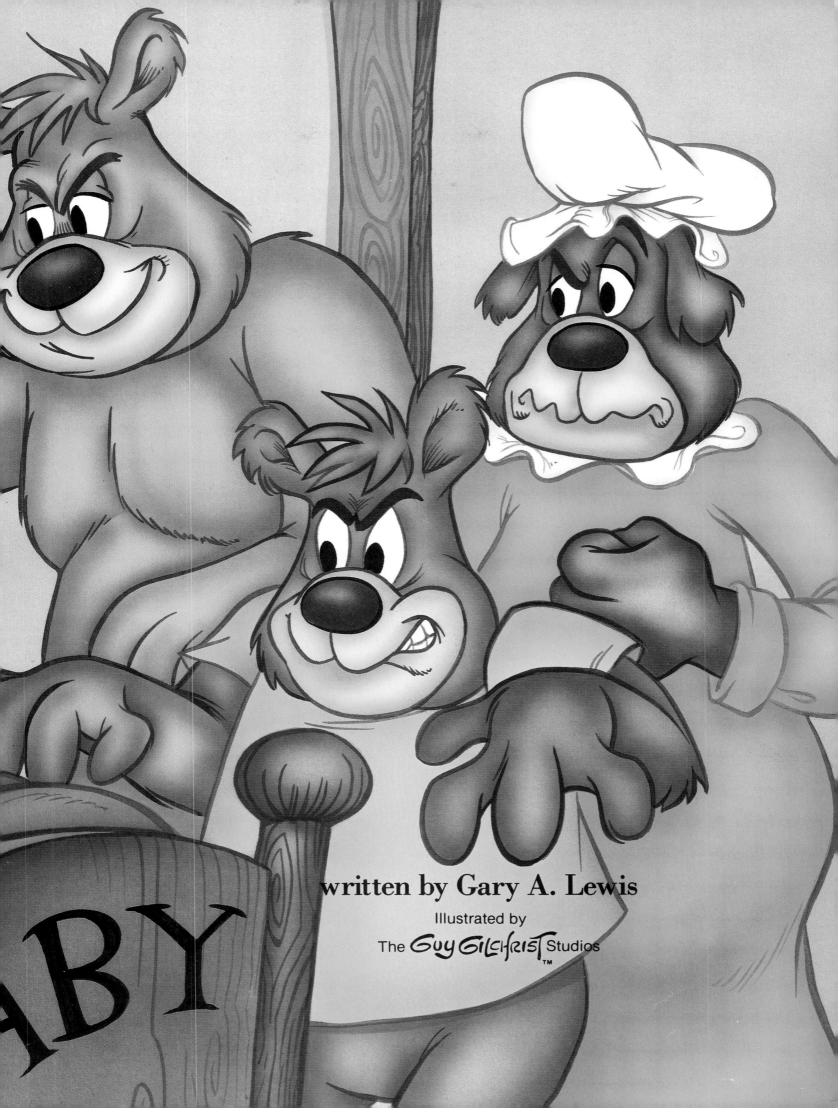

written by Gary A. Lewis

Illustrated by
The *Guy Gilchrist* Studios
™

"Owwwwwoooooo!"

"Uh…wh-wh-what's that?"

Elmer Fudd sat shivering in his tent as a lonely howling sound filled the night. He had gone rabbit hunting, and was camping out in the woods.

"Ooooh. What a fwightening sound," he thought. "I wish I had some company. It's no fun being all by myself."

That's when Bugs Bunny popped up—right in the middle of Elmer's tent. "Eh…what's up, Doc?" said Bugs, gnawing on a carrot.

"It's that sound," Elmer told him. "It sounds wike a…a…wolf."

"Well, whaddaya expect in the woods? Granny?" Bugs asked.

"If that noise keeps up, I won't ever get any sweep," Elmer sighed.

"Hey, look, Doc. Why don't I tell you a little bedtime story?" Bugs suggested. "That should do the trick!"

"All wight," Elmer agreed. "What stowy are you going to tell me?"

"How's about 'Little Red Riding Hood'? Bugs asked.
"Okay. Widdle Wed Widing Hood," Elmer agreed.
"I think that's what I said," said Bugs.

Once upon a time, there was a girl who was known as Little Red Riding Hood.

Now, Little Red Riding Hood had an old grandmother who lived alone in the woods. And one day, Little Red Riding Hood—or Red, as she was called—decided to visit her granny.

So she baked a cake, covered it with a checkered napkin, put it in a picnic basket, and set out on her way.

13

Red had only been in the forest for a few minutes when she met up with a rabbit.

"What's in the basket, Doc?" the rabbit asked.

"That's Red, not Doc," Little Red Riding Hood replied. "This isn't 'Snow White and the Seven Dwarfs,' you know. And it's a carrot cake. I'm taking it to my dear old granny, who lives in these woods."

THIS WAY TO GRANNY'S HOUSE!

"Oh, yeah. Granny." The rabbit nodded. "You know," he went on, "if I were you, I'd watch out. A big, bad wolf has been seen around these parts, and he just loves carrot cake. Why don't you leave the cake with me for safekeeping?"

"I think I'll take it with me, thanks all the same," said Red.

"In that case," the rabbit replied, "I'll go with you."

Meanwhile, the big, bad wolf had decided to pay a visit to Granny's too. He was a very hungry wolf, and he thought that a nice granny might be just the thing to fill up his rumbling tummy.

Unfortunately, Granny had gone out. So the wolf decided to make himself at home.

When Little Red Riding Hood got to Granny's house, she knocked at the door.

"It is I, Granny—Little Red Riding Hood," she called. "I've brought you a carrot cake. There's a rabbit here, too. He says he knows you."

When the wolf heard the knocking at the door, he had a brilliant idea. He had been waiting for Granny for a while, and he had gotten even hungrier. A Little Red Riding Hood and a rabbit would make a tasty supper.

Quick as a flash, the wolf jumped into Granny's nightgown and lacy bonnet and hopped into Granny's bed. Then he called out in a croaking kind of voice.

"Come in, dear," he said. "I have a bit of a cold, so I'm in the bedroom. Oh, and bring the rabbit with you."

"Hello, Granny," said Red, coming over to the bed. "You do sound terrible. Here's the cake."

"Why don't you go get some plates and forks," wheezed the wolf. "You can leave the rabbit here."

"Don't forget the napkins," said the rabbit.

"Dear me," said the rabbit, looking at the wolf. "What big eyes you have, Granny."

"The better to see you with, my dear," the wolf replied.

"And what big ears you have," the rabbit went on.

"The better to hear you with, my dear," said the wolf.

"And what big teeth you have," said Red, coming into the room with the plates and silverware.

"Put that down right on the table," the wolf told her. "The better to eat you with, my dears!" And the wolf jumped out of bed, throwing off Granny's nightgown.

"You're not my Granny!" said Little Red Riding Hood.

"How did you guess?" replied the wolf. "I'm the big, bad wolf, and I'm going to eat you both up!"

"Don't be silly," said the rabbit. "Nobody's eating anyone around here." And he bopped the wolf over the head with a cake plate.

The wolf stumbled out of the house with a terrible headache. Just as he did, Granny came home from her fishing trip.

"Get away from my house, you big, bad wolf, you!" she shouted. "I don't want you treading on my flower beds!"

The wolf raced off into the forest.

"Oh, Granny!" said Red. "I'm so glad you're safe. That big, bad wolf almost ate up all the carrot cake—and me and the rabbit, too!"

"What's that? A wabbit? Granny stared over her spectacles.
"Hmmm. And I was thinking of making wabbit stew for supper."
"Uh, I hate to eat and run," said the rabbit. "But…bye, Doc!"

That was the last anyone saw of the big, bad wolf in *that* part of the forest. But some folks say that he's still around somewhere, looking for his supper.

And so is Granny.

"You mean that wolf might still be around somewhere?" Elmer hid inside his sleeping bag. "Wooking for his supper?"

"That's what the story said, Doc," said Bugs.

"Did you hear something?" Elmer whispered. "I thought I heard a noise wight outside."

"Yeah, Doc," said Bugs. "Sounds like a bear to me."

"A *bear*?" Elmer gasped.

"Yep. And that reminds me of another story." Bugs chewed his carrot. "You want me to tell it to you?"

"Okay," said Elmer.

"Well, Doc," said Bugs. "This story is called, 'Bugs Bunny and the Three Bears'."

""Thwee Bears'?" said Elmer. "Do you weally think there are *thwee* bears out there?"

"Naw," said Bugs. "That's just the name of the story."

Once upon a time, there were three bears—a papa bear, a mama bear, and a baby bear. They lived in a cozy little house in the woods.

The three bears were hungry for supper. But there was nothing to eat in the pantry except for some moldy old carrots.

"I'm hungry!" said Baby Bear.

"Be quiet!" shouted Papa Bear. "Can't you see I'm thinking?"

Papa Bear thought and thought and thought. Finally, he had an idea.

"I've got it!" said Papa Bear. "Remember the story of the three bears? Well, why can't we do the same thing? We'll make some porridge, and pretend to go out for a walk. But when Goldilocks goes up to bed—wham! Goldilocks stew!"

"But Papa!" said Mama Bear. "We haven't any porridge for Goldilocks—only these old carrots."

"Well, then, make carrot soup! Make carrot soup!" cried Papa Bear. "Do I have to do *all* the thinking around here?"

43

After Mama Bear made the carrot soup, the three bears sat at the table.

"Now, say your lines," said Papa Bear.

"Oh," said Mama Bear. "My soup...I mean, my porridge...is too hot."

"My porridge is too hot," said Papa Bear.

"Uh...somebody's been sleeping in my bed!" said Baby Bear. "Uh, no. I mean, my porridge is too hot, too!"

"Now," said Mama Bear, "let's all go for a walk, and when we return, the porridge will be just right."

44

45

But the three bears didn't really go for a walk at all. Instead, they hid in the house, waiting for Goldilocks.

Meanwhile, somewhere in the forest, the delicious smell of carrot soup reached the hole of a particular rabbit.

"Mmmmm," said the rabbit, walking into the Bears' house and sitting down at the table. He tasted the first bowl of carrot soup. "This soup is too hot," he said.

Then he tasted the second bowl of carrot soup. "This soup is too cold," he said.

The bears, who had snuck back into the house, stood over the rabbit, about to pounce.

49

The rabbit was just about to taste the third bowl when he noticed something was wrong.

Mama and Papa Bear hit the floor, pretending to be bear rugs. They were determined to trick the rabbit.

Thud! Double Thud!!

51

"Mmmm," said the rabbit after he had finished all his soup. "I think I'll sit down for awhile on these nice, cozy bear rugs."

"Ouch!" said Baby Bear. He's sitting on my ears."

"Shhh!" hissed Papa Bear. "He'll hear you!"

"Now I'm really sleepy," the rabbit said after sitting there for a few minutes. "I think I'll go upstairs and lie down."

"Hey, Papa! He's going—" said Baby Bear.

"Shhh!" hissed Papa Bear. "Be quiet. It's all going exactly as we planned."

In the bedroom, the rabbit sat on the first bed. "This bed is too hard," he said.

Then he sat on the second bed. "This bed is too soft," he said.

Finally, he sat on the third bed. "This bed is just right," he said. "I think I'll get some shut-eye."

"Now, let's get that rabbit!" said Papa Bear. "And don't forget your lines!"

54

Papa Bear opened the bedroom door.
"Oh! Somebody's been sleeping in my bed!" said Mama Bear.
"Oh! Somebody's been sleeping in my bed!" said Papa Bear.
"Oh! Somebody's been sleeping in my bed!" said Baby Bear.
"And here he is still sleeping in my bed!"

"Eh, what's up, Doc?" said the rabbit. Then he sat up in bed and stared at Mama Bear.

"Don't move!" he said. "Your eyes. Your lips. Why, you're bee-yoo-ti-ful!"

He hopped out of bed. Papa Bear and Baby Bear jumped toward the rabbit. But Mama Bear stopped them.

"Wait!" she cried. "Don't you dare lay a hand on him, you brutes!"

The three bears never got their supper after all. But that was the last time the rabbit ever visited that particular house again—carrot soup or no carrot soup.